Franny K. Stein
MAD SCIENTIST

LUNCH WALKS AMONG US

JIM BENTON

SCHOLASTIC INC.

New York Toronto London Auckland Sydney
Mexico City New Delhi Hong Kong Buenos Aires

ISBN 0-439-69262-8

12 11 10 9 8 7 6 5 4 3 2 1   4 5 6 7 8 9/0

Printed in the U.S.A.   40

First Scholastic printing, September 2004

Book design by Dan Potash
The text for this book is set in Captain Kidd.
The illustrations for this book are rendered in pen and ink.

Franny K. Stein

MAD SCIENTIST

LUNCH WALKS AMONG US

For
Griffin,
Summer,
and Mary K

CONTENTS

1. Franny's House 1

2. Franny's Room 5

3. New at School 9

4. A Proposal 17

5. The Experiment Begins 23

6. Back at the Lab 35

7. Making Monsters 37

8. A Transformed Franny 55

9. Lunch Doesn't Agree with Me 61

10. That's No Jack-o'-Lantern 69

11. It's Mad Science Time 79

12. Ham, I Am 83

13. The Final Inning 87

14. Easy Come, Easy Go 93

15. Back to the Grind 95

16. Weird, but I Still Like Them 99

Franny K. Stein

MAD SCIENTIST

LUNCH WALKS AMONG US

CHAPTER ONE

FRANNY'S HOUSE

The Stein family lived in the pretty pink house with lovely purple shutters down at the end of Daffodil Street. Everything about the house was bright and cheery. Everything, that is, except the upstairs bedroom with the tiny round window.

That room belonged to Franny K. Stein, and she liked to keep it dark, and spooky, and creepy.

Every few days her mother would come in and redecorate Franny's bedroom with daisies, and lilacs, and pictures of lovely horses. It would always look so sweet and pretty.

But by the very next day Franny would somehow manage to make it look dark, and creepy, and spooky again. That was how she liked it—like a dungeon, complete with giant spiders and bats.

"Bats! Where does she get bats?" her mother would ask when she saw Franny's room. "Is there a bat store around here or something?"

Of course there wasn't a bat store around. The bats just kept showing up. The bats liked Franny's room, and Franny liked the bats.

"They're like rats with pterodactyl wings," she'd say. "What's not to like?"

CHAPTER TWO
FRANNY'S ROOM

Franny's bedroom was really something special. It had big steaming test tubes, strange bubbling beakers, and a whole bunch of crackling electrical gizmos that Franny had made all by herself.

Franny's room also had a giant tarantula cage, a snake house, and a tank where she raised a special breed of flying piranha. She couldn't imagine why anybody would want daisies and lilacs when they could have poison ivy and Venus flytraps.

"There's no comparison," she'd say, ducking one of her flying piranha.

Franny thought her room was so great, and
so wonderful, and so perfect for her that she
almost never wanted to leave it. But she had to,
of course, for things like going outside, eating
dinner, going to school, and using the bathroom.

Which is something Franny really liked to do.

Whoops. That didn't sound right. It was going to *school* that Franny really liked.

CHAPTER THREE
NEW AT SCHOOL

Franny and her family had just moved to the house at the end of Daffodil Street, and she was new at school. She liked her teacher, Miss Shelly. She thought she would like the other kids, too. But they really weren't very friendly toward Franny.

The other kids weren't mean; they just had never known anybody like Franny.

Nobody else had a jump rope like Franny's.

Franny's lunches didn't look like the other kids' lunches either.

And when they played hide-and-seek, no one could find her.

Franny could tell that the other kids were afraid of her, and that made her sad, because she really did want to make friends.

Her teacher, Miss Shelly, noticed what was happening. And one day she asked Franny to stay after class.

CHAPTER FOUR
A PROPOSAL

Miss Shelly was the nicest, smartest teacher Franny had ever had. Franny used to think that if only she dressed differently and wore her hair another way, she would be perfect.

"You're a wonderful student," Miss Shelly said.

"Thank you," Franny said. "I like school. Especially science. Especially the gooey parts of science."

"I like the gooey parts too," Miss Shelly said, and they both laughed.

"I'm a mad scientist, you know," Franny whispered.

"That must be very rewarding," Miss Shelly said, but she didn't really believe that Franny was a real-life mad scientist. Franny could tell.

"But I wonder if you might be a little lonely sometimes," Miss Shelly continued.

"I am lonely, sometimes," Franny admitted. "But I don't understand the other kids, and I don't know how to make friends with them."

"I think you can figure it out," said Miss Shelly. "You're smart."

Franny folded her arms. "I don't know, Miss Shelly..."

"Think of it as an experiment," Miss Shelly said.

Franny's eyes lit up. A wide grin crawled across her face. An experiment was the one thing she just could not resist, and Miss Shelly knew it.

"The experiment"—Franny pointed into
the air the way mad scientists do when they
think about conducting an experiment—
"begins tomorrow."

CHAPTER FIVE
THE EXPERIMENT BEGINS

The next day Franny came to school prepared to start her experiment. Before class she observed some of the girls playing with dolls. Franny was delighted. She knew about dolls.

She loved dolls. In fact she loved them so much that she had even made some special modifications to the ones she had at home.

Chompolina

FASHION DOLL BY
F.K. STEIN

CHOMPOLINA'S
STEEL TEETH
CAN EASILY MUNCH
THE HEADS OFF OTHER DOLLS!

SUPER DANGEROUS!

Oozette

CUDDLY DOLL
BY F.K. STEIN

OOZETTE GUSHES
STICKY GUNK
WHENEVER YOU
HUG HER! ♥

25

She was just about to tell the girls how Chompolina could bite the heads off their dolls when she noticed something. Their dolls were all kind of . . . sweet, and pretty. They all had long hair and flowery dresses. Not a single one of them oozed uck. They didn't ooze anything.

Franny made a note to herself: *Pretty,
non-head-biting dolls*, it said. *And less oozing.*

At lunchtime Franny sat down at a table with a bunch of kids. She was getting ready to take out her exquisitely delicious crab ravioli in pumpkin sauce when she made another observation.

Peanut butter and jelly sandwiches on her left, lunch-meat sandwiches on her right. As far as Franny's eyes could see was a carpet of soft, white, squishy sandwiches.

No casseroles, no stews, no shish kebabs; just sandwiches.

"Is this all they ever eat?" she whispered to herself. And she made another note: *Squashy sandwiches,* it said. Franny stuffed her lunch into the trash.

During recess the kids decided to play softball. "I have the ball," one of them said.

"But we need a bat," another one said.

A bat! Franny thought. *Finally. Something I
understand!* She reached into her backpack to
get one.

Just then a little boy ran past her with a baseball bat. "Batter up!" he shouted.

"Hmmm," said Franny. "There's more than *one* kind of bat."

As her classmates started playing, she took out her notebook and made another note: *A bat can also be a big stick you use to hit things*, she wrote.

After school Franny picked up her backpack
full of customized dolls, and spiders, and notes,
and bats, and headed home to analyze the data
she had gathered that day.

CHAPTER SIX

BACK AT THE LAB

Back in her room Franny looked over her notes. She made some calculations and puzzled over her findings.

"Nice kids," she said finally. "Kind of boring, but really nice."

That night Franny dreamed about how
much fun it would have been to play dolls with
those girls or to trade sandwiches at lunch.
Even softball looked like fun, in spite of the
fact that they used the kind of bat that didn't
have cute, veiny wings.

CHAPTER SEVEN
MAKING MONSTERS

Early the next morning, as she was getting ready for school, Franny pulled down her copy of *A Treasury of Monster-Making Techniques* and turned to the chapter on transformations. In particular she studied the part that explained how to transform a little girl mad scientist into something else.

FRANNY'S BOOK ON
MONSTER MAKING

Carefully cut on the dotted lines on
JUST THE NEXT TWO PAGES!

Flip the sections back and forth and see what
the recipe calls for to construct each
particular monster you create.

WARNING
We assume no responsibility if you actually
create a real monster and it destroys your
city and eats your stuff.

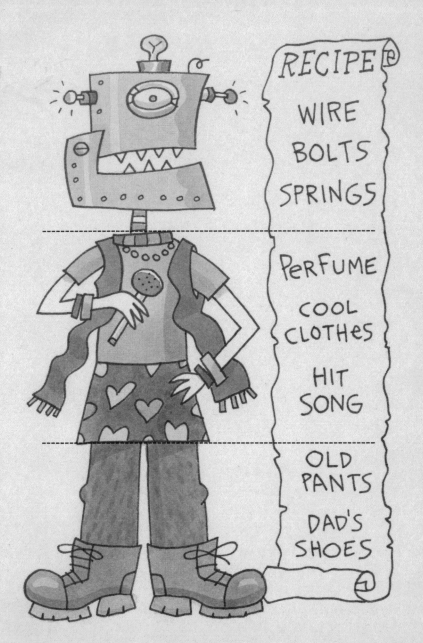

RECIPE

SHAMPOO

BLUSH

LIPSTICK

ZOMBIE
BODY

STINKY
VEST

WORMS

BALLOONS

POPCORN

COTTON
CANDY

41

RECIPE
ZOMBIE HEAD
LIGHTNING

ROACH BUTTS
SPIDER LEGS

DANCE LESSONS
CHUNKY HEELS

43

"I know just what to do," she said, and she began combining honey, vanilla jelly beans, and pink soda. She poured the formula into a tall, pretty glass decorated with a happy sheep holding a puppy wearing diapers.

"Ugh," she said. "How cute can you get?"

She put the mixture into one of her inventions, and programmed in her notes. The machine began to hum and shake, and buzz and bake, and then finally it binged, just like a microwave when your microwave popcorn is ready.

Franny gazed at the potion. She held her
nose and drank it. She ran to the mirror and
watched a strange transformation take place.

FRANNY TRANSFORMS

Carefully cut on the dotted lines on
JUST THE VERY NEXT PAGE!

Flip the sections and watch,
in horror, how Franny
transforms.

When Franny came downstairs to breakfast, her mom took one look at her and dropped her toast. Her dad choked on his coffee. Her brother's eyes almost popped out of his head.

"Franny," her Mother said, "you look so...nice."

Franny did look nice. Her hair was cute. Her dress was pretty. Her shoes were adorable. She didn't really look like Franny anymore, but she looked nice—kind of.

"Thanks, Mom," she said. "Here's a description of something I'd like prepared for lunch. It's strange, and horribly exotic, but I'd appreciate it if you could give it a try."

Her mom looked at the recipe that Franny had given her. "This says 'jelly and peanut butter between white bread slices,'" she said. "I'm pretty sure I can make this, Franny. I've been making it for years."

"Excellent," Franny said, and she rubbed her hands together in a mad-scientist way.

CHAPTER EIGHT

A TRANSFORMED FRANNY

Before school Franny met some of the girls from her class. Franny had a modified Chompolina with her.

Now Chompolina played happy music and squirted perfume and glitter and came with her own nail polish and a rainbow-colored unicorn with a long tail you could braid.

The other girls loved Chompolina and crowded around her.

Franny thought it was fun playing with the girls, but deep down she missed the old Chompolina.

At lunchtime Franny pulled out her PBJ sandwich. The peanut butter had been artfully smoothed, and the jelly had been applied equally from one corner to the other. The bread was so blazingly white that Franny needed sunglasses to look at it. Her mom had even trimmed the crusts, and the other kids, noticing this, smiled with approval.

Franny took a bite and found it to be totally, completely, and incredibly … average, uninteresting, and no big deal. She had expected so much more.

But her experiment seemed to be working, so she finished the mushy sandwich.

At recess Franny suggested they play soft-ball. She consulted her notes quickly and added, "I think it best we use a ball instead of a skull, or giant squid eyeball, or something gruesome like that."

The other kids were a bit puzzled, but they agreed.

Franny had fun playing with them, but deep down she knew the game would have been much more fun with a skull or giant squid eyeball.

After school the kids all said good-bye and a few even asked her to come over to their houses and play. It was great to be asked, but Franny had to hurry straight home and analyze her day. She was happy. The other kids liked her, even if it was only a *transformed* her.

CHAPTER NINE

LUNCH DOESN'T AGREE WITH ME

The next day at school, while the kids were doing their math problems, Miss Shelly took Franny over to one side and talked to her.

"How's the experiment going?" she asked.

"It's great. I understand them, and I think we're becoming friends. They seem to like me better if I just go along with the things they like."

"Are you sure that's for the best?" Miss Shelly asked.

"Well, that's what the data seem to suggest," Franny said, and showed Miss Shelly some graphs to back it up.

"But I like the real you." Miss Shelly was about to continue, when a piercing scream tore through the room.

"The trash can!" a little girl shrieked. "It's moving!"

Franny's mad scientist brain raced. That was the trash can in which she had dumped her crab ravioli in pumpkin sauce two days ago. But an old lunch, all by itself, was not enough to start a paranormal reaction.

"Who else put something in that can?"
Franny said.

"I spit out my gum in there," one girl said.

"I threw a pair of old gym shoes in there,"
another boy said.

"I saw the janitor dump some trash in
there," another girl said.

"Egad," said Franny. "That was close. Well,
as long as NOBODY put any unstable industrial
waste in there, we should be fine."

"Oh, yeah," said one little boy. "I forgot. I
put some unstable industrial waste in there."

"Gadzooks!" Franny shouted. "That is the
exact formula for a Giant Monstrous Fiend."

The other kids looked at her. They looked scared, not just of the mention of a Giant Monstrous Fiend, although the prospect of a Giant Monstrous Fiend was no comfort. They were also afraid of Franny. They were looking at her the way they used to, before they had become her good friends.

"I mean," Franny stammered, "that's what I would think if I was a weird mad scientist-type little girl, which, of course, I'm not."

They all smiled at her again.

Just then the trash can erupted like a volcano. As the smoke settled, the kids saw, for the first time, the type of Giant Monstrous Fiend that a mad scientist–type girl would have predicted.

CHAPTER TEN
THAT'S NO JACK-O'-LANTERN

The Giant Monstrous Fiend stood there chewing gum and breathing angrily. Its head was a pumpkin, and its body looked like a crab's. It was wearing the old shoes, and it was just dripping with industrial waste.

Franny hoped it would just jump out the window and go away.

And, to her surprise, the Pumpkin-Crab Monster jumped out the window and went away.

Unfortunately it grabbed Miss Shelly before it left. With a crash and a scream, the Pumpkin-Crab Monster and her teacher were gone.

The kids just stood there. They didn't know how to help. A few tried crying. A few tried screaming. One tried wetting his pants, although later on he admitted he had no idea why he thought that might help.

Some of Franny's new friends hugged her and shrieked, but Franny didn't shriek.

Franny *thought*.

Out the window the Pumpkin-Crab Monster was climbing the flagpole with Miss Shelly.

There was no way that Miss Shelly was going to get away from that monster thing. It was holding her tight, and it was climbing higher and higher.

Franny looked at her friends. She really liked them, and she was happy they liked her. She had hoped they would always be her friends, but still she knew what she had to do. Franny reached into her backpack and pulled out a vial. It said ANTIDOTE on it.

"Uh, guys," she said gently. "If you all get your lunches, I think I know what we might be able to do."

The kids ignored her. They just ran around in little circles, getting more and more scared and confused.

"Guys, really. I think I know what we need." Franny spoke a little louder this time, but they still ignored her.

"We need a fireman," one girl said.

"We need a superhero," one boy said.

"We need dry pants," said you-know-who.

Franny stood up. Outside, lightning cracked.

"What we need," she said, "is a mad scientist. WHICH I AM." She uncorked the antidote and drank it.

She began to cough and sputter and spit. She fell on the ground and scrunched down in a little ball. She stood up and felt herself return to normal.

Franny, the little girl mad scientist, was back.

CHAPTER ELEVEN

IT'S MAD SCIENCE TIME

Franny looked at the kids. They looked even more afraid of her now than they ever had before. She thought about trying to be sweet or less scary, but that just wasn't going to get things done.

"Do as I command!" she said in her most scary mad scientist voice. "Go get your lunches!"

The kids stopped running in circles and ran to get their lunches. Mad scientists, even when they're only four feet tall, can be very persuasive.

"Put the bread in one pile and the lunch meat in another," she barked.

The kids did as they were told and quickly disassembled their sandwiches.

Franny was busy examining the bottom of the trash can. "I think there's just enough of this unstable industrial waste left to do the trick."

Franny worked fast. She told the kids exactly how to arrange the lunch meat and how to get the bread ready.

They were afraid, but they did what she said, and they did it quickly.

Being the only mad scientist around, she was the expert on unstable industrial waste, so she took care of that personally.

Then Franny pulled a needle and thread from her backpack.

"This will require absolute silence," she said, and the kids watched her begin stitching the lunch meat together.

Franny worked quickly as the kids watched in terror, occasionally handing her additional slices of salami or bologna when she so instructed.

They knew they were watching something not of this world, something that no human eyes had ever seen before, and in that moment the pants wetter decided to let loose one more time.

CHAPTER TWELVE

HAM, I AM

Finally Franny walked solemnly across the
room and washed snips of ham and smears
of mustard off her hands in the sink.

She sighed a deep, satisfied sigh and turned
to gaze on her creation.

There, standing motionless in the middle of the classroom, was a giant monster thing made entirely of glistening, delicious bologna, salami, pickle loaf, and ham.

The time had come to provide this creature with the awesome power source it would need to come alive.

Franny grasped its salami nose and slid two batteries up its nostrils. "Awaken," she commanded. The creature's eyes slowly opened. It growled and looked at Franny. The kids clung to one another in fear.

"The flagpole," Franny ordered, and the creature began walking stiffly toward the wall. With a mighty punch it smashed its way through and headed outside.

"Bread!" Franny yelled, and the kids, follow-
ing Franny's plan, began pushing the pile of
bread over to the base of the flagpole.

The Lunch-Meat Creature grabbed the pole
and shook it. Miss Shelly screamed, and the
kids gasped.

"Shake harder!" Franny commanded.

The Lunch-Meat Creature shook and shook
until finally the Pumpkin-Crab Monster
dropped Miss Shelly.

CHAPTER THIRTEEN
THE FINAL INNING

Franny watched calmly as Miss Shelly fell toward the ground, screaming. Then, with the loudest *puff* sound anybody had ever heard, Miss Shelly fell right into the big, squishy pile of white bread, completely unharmed.

Franny turned to the Lunch-Meat Creature. "Now, my lunch-meat abomination, go get that pumpkin-headed creep."

The Lunch-Meat Creature grabbed the flag-pole tightly and pulled until bologna-flavored sweat dripped off its forehead.

Finally, with a monstrous groan, the Lunch-Meat Creature ripped the flagpole right out of the ground, causing a very angry Pumpkin-Crab Monster to fall and hit the pavement with a ground-shaking crash.

The Pumpkin-Crab Monster got to its feet and growled. It began stomping toward the kids.

It was almost on top of them when Franny, the only kid that did not look worried, calmly whistled.

Suddenly a cloud of bats flew down from the sky and grabbed the Pumpkin-Crab Monster by the arms.

"Batter up," she said.

The bats flew as fast as they could with the Pumpkin-Crab Monster, and they headed right for the Lunch-Meat Creature, who had the flagpole up on its shoulder.

The bats dropped their burden just in time for the Lunch-Meat Creature to bring the pole around like a giant baseball bat and connect with the Pumpkin-Crab Monster as if it were a giant, stinky softball.

With a loud crack it went hurtling off into the sky, never to be seen, or heard from, again.

"Home run!" shouted Franny.

Then Franny turned around and saw the
shocked and horrified kids huddled around an
equally shocked and horrified Miss Shelly.

They looked more scared of her than ever.

Franny had the sad, sinking feeling that
she had saved the day but had lost all of her
friends.

CHAPTER FOURTEEN
EASY COME, EASY GO

"I, uh, could probably take the Lunch-Meat Creature apart and make your sandwiches again," Franny offered weakly.

"And sorry about the flagpole, Miss Shelly," Franny said. "And about the wall my Lunch-Meat Creature smashed through.

"Sorry about your pants, kid," she said to the boy who had wet his pants and who was now getting pretty tired of people talking about it.

The kids all just stood there, trembling.
They didn't say a thing.

Franny turned away and walked home,
sadder and lonelier than ever before.

CHAPTER FIFTEEN
BACK TO THE GRIND

The next day Franny went to school as herself. There was no reason to pretend anymore. The kids were afraid of her and probably always would be. Worse yet, Miss Shelly was probably afraid of her now too.

Franny opened the door to her classroom slowly. Suddenly a giant cheer went up from the kids inside.

"Hooray for Franny!" they yelled. "Hooray, hooray, hooray!"

Franny looked around, stunned. The kids were all hugging her and thanking her for saving them.

"Thank you," Miss Shelly said and hugged her closest of all.

Franny was shocked. She fumbled over her words. "Uh, you're welcome."

"Your monster fixed the flagpole and the wall," Miss Shelly said. "And it did such a great job, the principal wants to hire it to work here."

The Lunch-Meat Monster waved and grinned proudly.

"You're the coolest, Franny!" the kids shouted.

"You're not scared of me?" Franny asked.

"Well, it would be hard not to be a little scared. I mean, you did make a monster out of cold cuts," one girl said. "But still, you're our friend. And that makes it all okay."

"Friend!" Franny said. "Yeah, I am your friend. Just the way I am, just the way you are. Friends!"

CHAPTER SIXTEEN

WEIRD, BUT I STILL LIKE THEM

They didn't always like the same things, but they were all still friends after that. The other girls decided that Chompolina and Oozette actually *were* pretty fun.

And Franny learned how to enjoy an occasional peanut butter and jelly sandwich.

And together they figured out a way to play softball with both kinds of bats.

It was an unusual friendship, but a great one. And considering how experiments often end up for mad scientists, Franny thought this one had gone pretty darn well.